CHILDREN'S CLASSICS
EVERYMAN'S LIBRARY

Robert Browning

The Pied Piper
of
Hamelin

With Illustrations
by Kate Greenaway

EVERYMAN'S LIBRARY
CHILDREN'S CLASSICS

First published 1842
First included in Everyman's Library 1993

Design and typography © David Campbell Publishers Ltd., 1993

Book design by Barbara de Wilde, Carol Devine Carson and Peter B. Willberg

Five of Ernest H. Shepard's illustrations from *Dream Days* by Kenneth
Grahame are reprinted on the endpapers by permission of The Bodley Head,
London. The sixth illustration is by S.C. Hulme Beaman.

ISBN 1–85715–922–5

A CIP catalogue record for this book is available from the British Library

Published by David Campbell Publishers Ltd.,
79 Berwick Street, London W1V 3PF

Distributed by Random House (UK) Ltd.,
20 Vauxhall Bridge Road, London SW1V 2SA

Printed and bound in Germany by
Mohndruck Graphische Betriebe GmbH, Gütersloh

THE PIED PIPER
OF HAMELIN;

A Child's Story.

(written for, and inscribed to,
W. M. the younger.)

I.

HAMELIN Town's in Brunswick,
By famous Hanover city;
 The River Weser, deep and wide,
 Washes its wall on the southern side;
 A pleasanter spot you never spied;
But, when begins my ditty,
 Almost five hundred years ago,
 To see townsfolk suffer so
  From vermin, was a pity.

II.

Rats!
They fought the dogs, and killed the cats,
And bit the babies in the cradles,

And ate the cheeses out of the vats,

And licked the soup from the cook's own ladles,

Split open the kegs of salted sprats,
Made nests inside men's Sunday hats,

And even spoiled the women's chats,
By drowning their speaking
With shrieking and squeaking
In fifty different sharps and flats.

III.

At last the people in a body
　　To the Town Hall came flocking:
" 'Tis clear," cried they, "our Mayor's a noddy;
　　"And as for our Corporation—shocking

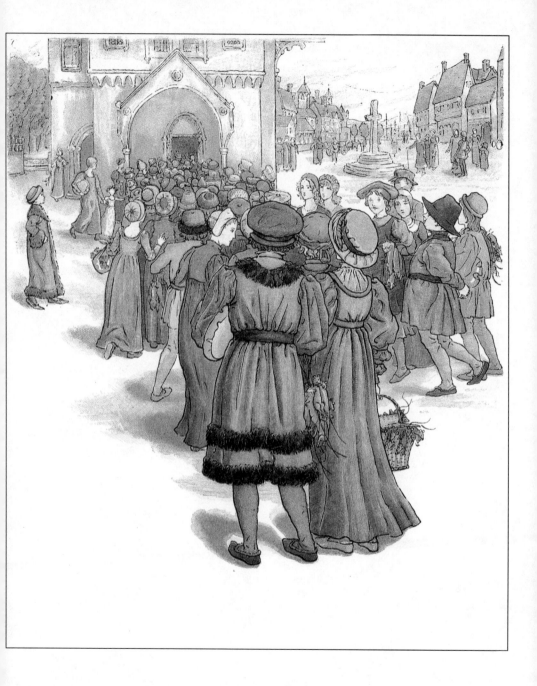

"To think we buy gowns lined with ermine
"For dolts that can't or won't determine
"What's best to rid us of our vermin!
"You hope, because you're old and obese,
"To find in the furry civic robe ease?
"Rouse up, Sirs! Give your brains a racking
"To find the remedy we're lacking,
"Or, sure as fate, we'll send you packing!"
  At this the Mayor and Corporation
  Quaked with a mighty consternation.

IV.

An hour they sate in council,
    At length the Mayor broke silence:
"For a guilder I'd my ermine gown sell;
    "I wish I were a mile hence!
"It's easy to bid one rack one's brain—
"I'm sure my poor head aches again
"I've scratched it so, and all in vain.
"Oh for a trap, a trap, a trap!"
  Just as he said this, what should hap

At the chamber door but a gentle tap?
"Bless us," cried the Mayor, "what's that?"
  (With the Corporation as he sat,
  Looking little though wondrous fat;
  Nor brighter was his eye, nor moister
  Than a too-long-opened oyster,
  Save when at noon his paunch grew mutinous
  For a plate of turtle green and glutinous)
"Only a scraping of shoes on the mat?
"Anything like the sound of a rat
"Makes my heart go pit-a-pat!

V.

"Come in!"—the Mayor cried, looking bigger:
  And in did come the strangest figure!
  His queer long coat from heel to head
  Was half of yellow and half of red;
  And he himself was tall and thin,
  With sharp blue eyes, each like a pin,
  And light loose hair, yet swarthy skin,
  No tuft on cheek nor beard on chin,
  But lips where smiles went out and in—
  There was no guessing his kith and kin!
  And nobody could enough admire
  The tall man and his quaint attire:
  Quoth one: "It's as my great-grandsire,
"Starting up at the Trump of Doom's tone,
"Had walked this way from his painted tombstone!"

VI.

He advanced to the council-table:
And, "Please your honours," said he, "I'm able,
"By means of a secret charm, to draw
"All creatures living beneath the sun,
"That creep, or swim, or fly, or run,
"After me so as you never saw!
"And I chiefly use my charm
"On creatures that do people harm,
"The mole, and toad, and newt, and viper;
"And people call me the Pied Piper."
  (And here they noticed round his neck
  A scarf of red and yellow stripe,
  To match with his coat of the self same cheque;

And at the scarf's end hung a pipe;
And his fingers, they noticed, were ever straying
As if impatient to be playing
Upon this pipe, as low it dangled
Over his vesture so old-fangled.)

"Yet," said he, "poor piper as I am.
"In Tartary I freed the Cham,
"Last June, from his huge swarms of gnats;
"I eased in Asia the Nizam
"Of a monstrous brood of vampire-bats:
"And, as for what your brain bewilders,
"If I can rid your town of rats
"Will you give me a thousand guilders?"
"One? fifty thousand!"—was the exclamation
  Of the astonished Mayor and Corporation.

VII.

Into the street the Piper stept,
    Smiling first a little smile,
As if he knew what magic slept
    In his quiet pipe the while;
Then, like a musical adept,
To blow the pipe his lips he wrinkled,
And green and blue his sharp eyes twinkled
Like a candle flame where salt is sprinkled;
And ere three shrill notes the pipe uttered,
You heard as if an army muttered;

And the muttering grew to a grumbling;
And the grumbling grew to a mighty rumbling;
And out of the houses the rats came tumbling:
Great rats, small rats, lean rats, brawny rats,
Brown rats, black rats, grey rats, tawny rats,
Grave old plodders, gay young friskers,

Fathers, mothers, uncles, cousins,
Cocking tails and pricking whiskers,
Families by tens and dozens,
Brothers, sisters, husbands, wives—
Followed the Piper for their lives.
From street to street he piped advancing,
And step for step they followed dancing,
Until they came to the river Weser
Wherein all plunged and perished
—Save one who, stout as Julius Cæsar,
Swam across and lived to carry
(As he the manuscript he cherished)
To Rat-land home his commentary,

Which was, "At the first shrill notes of the pipe,
"I heard a sound as of scraping tripe,
"And putting apples, wondrous ripe,
"Into a cider-press's gripe:
"And a moving away of pickle-tub boards,
"And a leaving ajar of conserve-cupboards,
"And the drawing the corks of train-oil-flasks,
"And a breaking the hoops of butter-casks;
"And it seemed as if a voice
"(Sweeter far than by harp or by psaltery
"(Is breathed) called out, Oh rats, rejoice!
"The world is grown to one vast drysaltery!
"So munch on, crunch on, take your nuncheon,
"Breakfast, supper, dinner, luncheon!
"And just as a bulky sugar-puncheon,
"All ready staved, like a great sun shone
"Glorious scarce an inch before me,
"Just as methought it said, Come, bore me!
"—I found the Weser rolling o'er me."

VIII.

You should have heard the Hamelin people
  Ringing the bells till they rocked the steeple;
"Go," cried the Mayor, "and get long poles!
"Pike out the nests and block up the holes!

"Consult with carpenters and builders,
"And leave in our town not even a trace
"Of the rats!"—when suddenly up the face
 Of the Piper perked in the market-place,
 With a, "First, if you please, my thousand guilders!"

IX.

A thousand guilders! The Mayor looked blue;
So did the Corporation too.
For council dinners made rare havock
With Claret, Moselle, Vin-de-Grave, Hock;
And half the money would replenish
Their cellar's biggest butt with Rhenish.
To pay this sum to a wandering fellow
With a gipsy coat of red and yellow!
"Beside," quoth the Mayor with a knowing wink,
"Our business was done at the river's brink;
"We saw with our eyes the vermin sink,
"And what's dead can't come to life, I think.
"So, friend, we're not the folks to shrink
"From the duty of giving you something for drink,
"And a matter of money to put in your poke;
"But, as for the guilders, what we spoke
"Of them, as you very well know, was in joke.
"Beside, our losses have made us thrifty;
"A thousand guilders! Come, take fifty!"

47

X.

The Piper's face fell, and he cried,
"No trifling! I can't wait, beside!
"I've promised to visit by dinner time
"Bagdat, and accept the prime
"Of the Head Cook's pottage, all he's rich in,
"For having left, in the Caliph's kitchen,
"Of a nest of scorpions no survivor—
"With him I proved no bargain-driver,
"With you, don't think I'll bate a stiver!
"And folks who put me in a passion
"May find me pipe to another fashion."

XI.

"How?" cried the Mayor, "d'ye think I'll brook
"Being worse treated than a Cook?
"Insulted by a lazy ribald
"With idle pipe and vesture piebald?
"You threaten us, fellow? Do your worst,
"Blow your pipe there till you burst!"

XII.

Once more he stept into the street;
    And to his lips again
Laid his long pipe of smooth straight cane;
    And ere he blew three notes (such sweet
Soft notes as yet musician's cunning
    Never gave the enraptured air)

There was a rustling, that seemed like a bustling

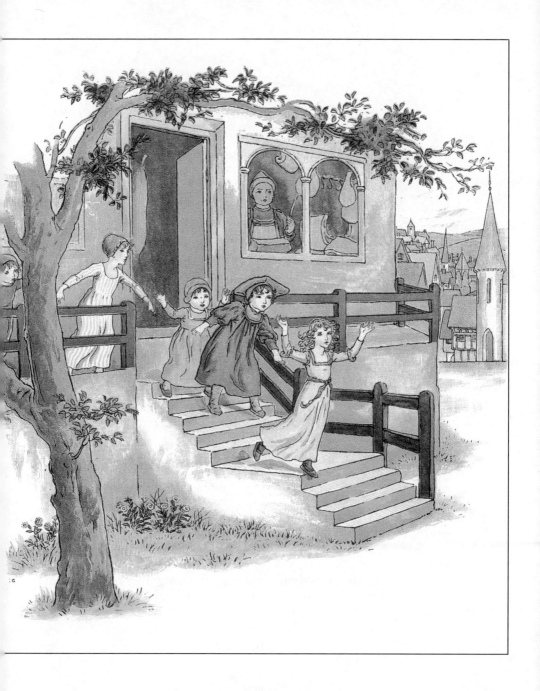

Of merry crowds justling at pitching and hustling.

Small feet were pattering, wooden shoes clattering,

Little hands clapping, and little tongues chattering,

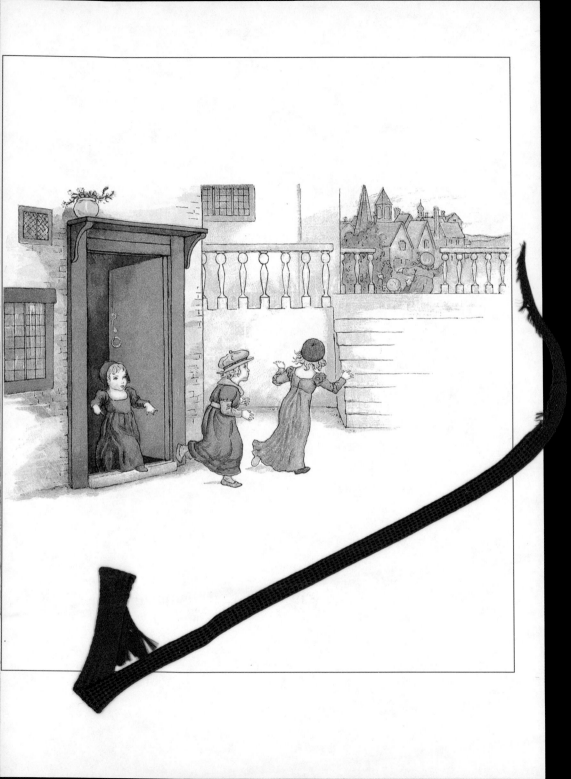

And, like fowls in a farm-yard when barley is scattering,

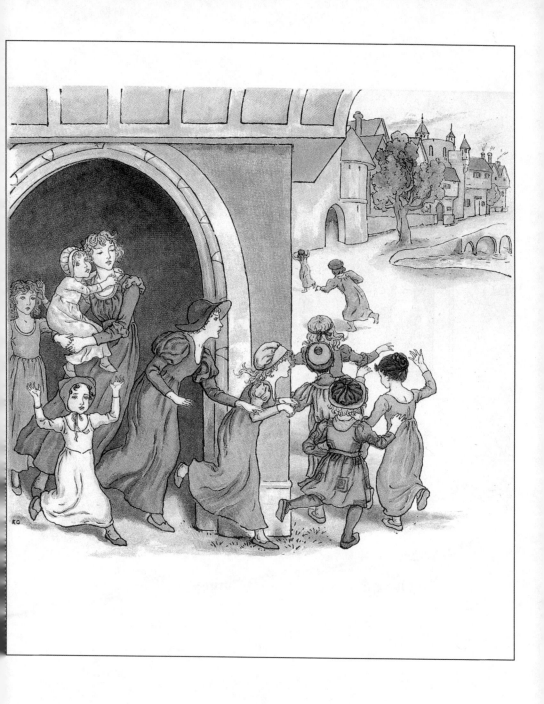

Out came the children running.

All the little boys and girls,

With rosy cheeks and flaxen curls,

And sparkling eyes and teeth like pearls,

Tripping and skipping, ran merrily after

The wonderful music with shouting and laughter.

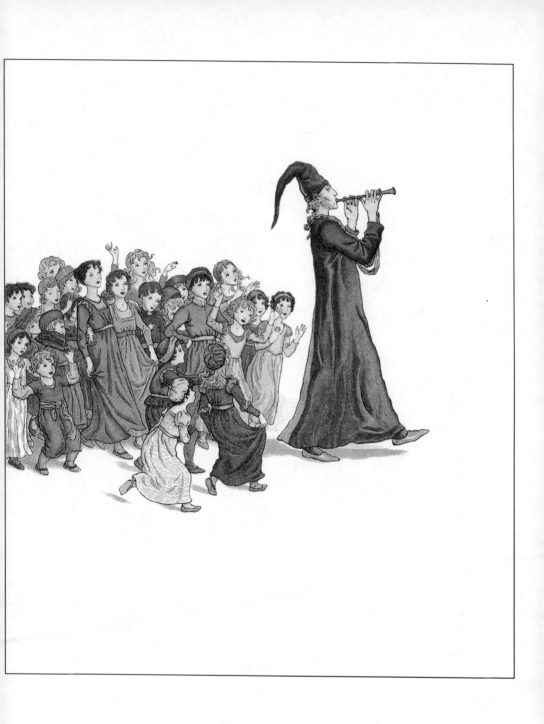

XIII.

The Mayor was dumb, and the Council stood
As if they were changed into blocks of wood,
Unable to move a step, or cry
To the children merrily skipping by—

And could only follow with the eye
That joyous crowd at the Piper's back.
But how the Mayor was on the rack,
And the wretched Council's bosoms beat,
As the Piper turned from the High Street
To where the Weser rolled its waters
Right in the way of their sons and daughters!
However he turned from South to West,
And to Koppelberg Hill his steps addressed,
And after him the children pressed;
Great was the joy in every breast.
"He never can cross that mighty top!
"He's forced to let the piping drop,
"And we shall see our children stop!"
When, lo, as they reached the mountain's side,
A wondrous portal opened wide,

As if a cavern was suddenly hollowed;
And the Piper advanced and the children followed,
And when all were in to the very last,
The door in the mountain side shut fast.
Did I say, all? No! One was lame,
And could not dance the whole of the way;
And in after years, if you would blame
His sadness, he was used to say,—
"It's dull in our town since my playmates left!
"I can't forget that I'm bereft
"Of all the pleasant sights they see,
"Which the Piper also promised me;
"For he led us, he said, to a joyous land,
"Joining the town and just at hand,

"Where waters gushed and fruit-trees grew,
"And flowers put forth a fairer hue,
"And everything was strange and new;
"The sparrows were brighter than peacocks here,
"And their dogs outran our fallow deer,
"And honey-bees had lost their stings,
"And horses were born with eagles' wings;
"And just as I became assured
"My lame foot would be speedily cured,
"The music stopped and I stood still,
"And found myself outside the Hill,
"Left alone against my will,
"To go now limping as before,
"And never hear of that country more!"

XIV.

Alas, alas for Hamelin!
    There came into many a burgher's pate
    A text which says, that Heaven's Gate
    Opes to the Rich at as easy rate
As the needle's eye takes a camel in!
The Mayor sent East, West, North, and South
To offer the Piper by word of mouth,
    Wherever it was men's lot to find him,
Silver and gold to his heart's content,
If he'd only return the way he went,
    And bring the children behind him.
But when they saw 'twas a lost endeavour,
And Piper and dancers were gone for ever,
They made a decree that lawyers never

Should think their records dated duly
If, after the day of the month and year,
These words did not as well appear,
"And so long after what happened here
    "On the Twenty-second of July,
"Thirteen hundred and Seventy-six:"
And the better in memory to fix
The place of the Children's last retreat,
They called it, the Pied Piper's Street—
Where any one playing on pipe or tabor
Was sure for the future to lose his labour.
Nor suffered they Hostelry or Tavern

To shock with mirth a street so solemn;
But opposite the place of the cavern
   They wrote the story on a column,
And on the Great Church Window painted
The same, to make the world acquainted
How their children were stolen away;
And there it stands to this very day.
And I must not omit to say
That in Transylvania there's a tribe
Of alien people that ascribe
The outlandish ways and dress
On which their neighbours lay such stress,
To their fathers and mothers having risen
Out of some subterraneous prison
Into which they were trepanned
Long time ago in a mighty band
Out of Hamelin town in Brunswick land,
But how or why, they don't understand.

XV.

So, Willy, let you and me be wipers
Of scores out with all men—especially pipers:
And, whether they pipe us free, from rats or from mice,
If we've promised them aught, let us keep our promise.

ROBERT BROWNING (1812–1889) was born in Camberwell, London, the son of a clerk in the Bank of England. The strongest influence on his education were the books in his father's extensive library, particularly the writings of Byron and Shelley. His dramatic poem *Paracelsus*, published in 1835, established his reputation and brought him the friendship of the actor-manager William Macready. When Macready's eldest son Willie was ill in bed, Browning wrote for the boy's entertainment the poem of *The Pied Piper*, a story he remembered from his own childhood. After its appearance in print in 1842, it became a children's classic, attracting new illustrators in every generation.

In 1846 Robert Browning married a fellow poet, Elizabeth Barrett, eloping with her to Italy where they lived until Elizabeth's death in 1861. He then returned to England to live with his only sister Sarianna, but later he went back to Italy, where he died at the Rezzonico Palace in Venice.

KATE GREENAWAY (1846–1901) was born in Hoxton, London, the daughter of a well-known engraver, John Greenaway. The happiest days of her childhood were spent in the country, at the village of Rolleston in Nottinghamshire, which was the inspiration for her very distinctive style of illustration. She showed her drawing talent early and after studying at Heatherley's and the Slade School of Art she held her first exhibition when she was only twenty-two. Ten years later the printer Edmund Evans, a friend of her father, engraved and published her collection of illustrated verses, *Under the Window*, which was an immediate commercial success. It was the first of many books that made her one of the great triumvirate (with Walter Crane and Randolph Caldecott) whose creations proved that quality picture books for children could be financially profitable.

John Ruskin was an admirer of Kate Greenaway's art and thought her illustrations for *The Pied Piper* the 'grandest thing' she had ever done. He wrote to her, 'You have really got through your rats with credit.'